THE PROPHET

The Books of

KAHLIL GIBRAN

"His power came from some great reservoir of spiritual life
else it could not have been so universal and so potent, but
the majesty and beauty of the language with which he clothed
it were all his own." — CLAUDE BRAGDON

The Madman · 1918

Twenty Drawings · 1919

The Forerunner · 1920

The Prophet · 1923

Sand and Foam · 1926

Jesus the Son of Man · 1928

The Earth Gods · 1931

The Wanderer · 1932

The Garden of the Prophet · 1933

Prose Poems · 1934

Nymphs of the Valley · 1948

Spirits Rebellious · 1948

A Tear and a Smile · 1950

∵

This Man from Lebanon —

A Study of Kahlil Gibran
by Barbara Young

PUBLISHED BY ALFRED A. KNOPF

THE PROPHET

BY

KAHLIL GIBRAN

NEW YORK · ALFRED A. KNOPF · MCMLII

Published September 1923
Reprinted fifty-four times
Fifty-sixth printing, September 1952

 THIS IS A BORZOI BOOK,
PUBLISHED BY ALFRED A. KNOPF, INC.

Manufactured in the United States of America

CONTENTS

THE PROPHET

THE TWELVE ILLUSTRATIONS
IN THIS VOLUME ARE RE-
PRODUCED FROM ORIGINAL
DRAWINGS BY THE AUTHOR

ALMUSTAFA, the chosen and the beloved, who was a dawn unto his own day, had waited twelve years in the city of Orphalese for his ship that was to return and bear him back to the isle of his birth.

And in the twelfth year, on the seventh day of Ielool, the month of reaping, he climbed the hill without the city walls and looked seaward; and he beheld his ship coming with the mist.

Then the gates of his heart were flung open, and his joy flew far over the sea. And he closed his eyes and prayed in the silences of his soul.

But as he descended the hill, a sadness came upon him, and he thought in his heart:

How shall I go in peace and without sorrow? Nay, not without a wound in the spirit shall I leave this city.

Long were the days of pain I have spent within its walls, and long were the nights of aloneness; and who can depart from his pain and his aloneness without regret?

Too many fragments of the spirit have I scattered in these streets, and too many are the children of my longing that walk naked among these hills, and I cannot withdraw from them without a burden and an ache.

It is not a garment I cast off this day, but a skin that I tear with my own hands.

Nor is it a thought I leave behind me, but a heart made sweet with hunger and with thirst.

Yet I cannot tarry longer.

The sea that calls all things unto her calls me, and I must embark.

For to stay, though the hours burn in the night, is to freeze and crystallize and be bound in a mould.

Fain would I take with me all that is here. But how shall I?

A voice cannot carry the tongue and

the lips that gave it wings. Alone must it seek the ether.

And alone and without his nest shall the eagle fly across the sun.

Now when he reached the foot of the hill, he turned again towards the sea, and he saw his ship approaching the harbour, and upon her prow the mariners, the men of his own land.

And his soul cried out to them, and he said:

Sons of my ancient mother, you riders of the tides,

How often have you sailed in my dreams. And now you come in my awakening, which is my deeper dream.

Ready am I to go, and my eagerness with sails full set awaits the wind.

Only another breath will I breathe in this still air, only another loving look cast backward,

And then I shall stand among you, a seafarer among seafarers.

And you, vast sea, sleepless mother,
Who alone are peace and freedom to
the river and the stream,
Only another winding will this stream
make, only another murmur in this glade,
And then shall I come to you, a boundless drop to a boundless ocean.

And as he walked he saw from afar men
and women leaving their fields and their
vineyards and hastening towards the city
gates.
And he heard their voices calling his
name, and shouting from field to field telling one another of the coming of his ship.

And he said to himself:
Shall the day of parting be the day of
gathering?
And shall it be said that my eve was in
truth my dawn?
And what shall I give unto him who
has left his plough in midfurrow, or to
him who has stopped the wheel of his
winepress?

10

Shall my heart become a tree heavy-laden with fruit that I may gather and give unto them?

And shall my desires flow like a fountain that I may fill their cups?

Am I a harp that the hand of the mighty may touch me, or a flute that his breath may pass through me?

A seeker of silences am I, and what treasure have I found in silences that I may dispense with confidence?

If this is my day of harvest, in what fields have I sowed the seed, and in what unremembered seasons?

If this indeed be the hour in which I lift up my lantern, it is not my flame that shall burn therein.

Empty and dark shall I raise my lantern,

And the guardian of the night shall fill it with oil and he shall light it also.

These things he said in words. But much in his heart remained unsaid. For he himself could not speak his deeper secret.

And when he entered into the city all the people came to meet him, and they were crying out to him as with one voice.

And the elders of the city stood forth and said:

Go not yet away from us.

A noontide have you been in our twilight, and your youth has given us dreams to dream.

No stranger are you among us, nor a guest, but our son and our dearly beloved.

Suffer not yet our eyes to hunger for your face.

And the priests and the priestesses said unto him:

Let not the waves of the sea separate us now, and the years you have spent in our midst become a memory.

You have walked among us a spirit,

and your shadow has been a light upon our faces.

Much have we loved you. But speech-less was our love, and with veils has it been veiled.

Yet now it cries aloud unto you, and would stand revealed before you.

And ever has it been that love knows not its own depth until the hour of separation.

And others came also and entreated him. But he answered them not. He only bent his head; and those who stood near saw his tears falling upon his breast.

And he and the people proceeded towards the great square before the temple.

And there came out of the sanctuary a woman whose name was Almitra. And she was a seeress.

And he looked upon her with exceeding tenderness, for it was she who had first sought and believed in him when he had been but a day in their city.

And she hailed him, saying:

Prophet of God, in quest of the uttermost, long have you searched the distances for your ship.

And now your ship has come, and you must needs go.

Deep is your longing for the land of your memories and the dwelling place of your greater desires; and our love would not bind you nor our needs hold you.

Yet this we ask ere you leave us, that you speak to us and give us of your truth.

And we will give it unto our children, and they unto their children, and it shall not perish.

In your aloneness you have watched with our days, and in your wakefulness you have listened to the weeping and the laughter of our sleep.

Now therefore disclose us to ourselves, and tell us all that has been shown you of that which is between birth and death.

And he answered,

People of Orphalese, of what can I

speak save of that which is even now moving within your souls?

Then said Almitra, Speak to us of Love.

And he raised his head and looked upon the people, and there fell a stillness upon them. And with a great voice he said:

When love beckons to you, follow him,

Though his ways are hard and steep.

And when his wings enfold you yield to him,

Though the sword hidden among his pinions may wound you.

And when he speaks to you believe in him,

Though his voice may shatter your dreams as the north wind lays waste the garden.

For even as love crowns you so shall he crucify you. Even as he is for your growth so is he for your pruning.

Even as he ascends to your height and

caresses your tenderest branches that quiver in the sun,

So shall he descend to your roots and shake them in their clinging to the earth.

Like sheaves of corn he gathers you unto himself.

He threshes you to make you naked.

He sifts you to free you from your husks.

He grinds you to whiteness.

He kneads you until you are pliant;

And then he assigns you to his sacred fire, that you may become sacred bread for God's sacred feast.

All these things shall love do unto you that you may know the secrets of your heart, and in that knowledge become a fragment of Life's heart.

But if in your fear you would seek only love's peace and love's pleasure,

Then it is better for you that you cover

your nakedness and pass out of love's threshing-floor,

Into the seasonless world where you shall laugh, but not all of your laughter, and weep, but not all of your tears.

Love gives naught but itself and takes naught but from itself.

Love possesses not nor would it be possessed;

For love is sufficient unto love.

When you love you should not say, "God is in my heart," but rather, "I am in the heart of God."

And think not you can direct the course of love, for love, if it finds you worthy, directs your course.

Love has no other desire but to fulfil itself.

But if you love and must needs have desires, let these be your desires:

To melt and be like a running brook that sings its melody to the night.

To know the pain of too much tenderness.

To be wounded by your own understanding of love;

And to bleed willingly and joyfully.

To wake at dawn with a winged heart and give thanks for another day of loving;

To rest at the noon hour and meditate love's ecstacy;

To return home at eventide with gratitude;

And then to sleep with a prayer for the beloved in your heart and a song of praise upon your lips.

Then Almitra spoke again and said,
And what of Marriage, master?

And he answered saying:

You were born together, and together you shall be forevermore.

You shall be together when the white wings of death scatter your days.

Aye, you shall be together even in the silent memory of God.

But let there be spaces in your togetherness,

And let the winds of the heavens dance between you.

Love one another, but make not a bond of love:

Let it rather be a moving sea between the shores of your souls.

Fill each other's cup but drink not from one cup.

Give one another of your bread but eat not from the same loaf.

Sing and dance together and be joyous, but let each one of you be alone,

Even as the strings of a lute are alone though they quiver with the same music.

Give your hearts, but not into each other's keeping.

For only the hand of Life can contain your hearts.

And stand together yet not too near together:

For the pillars of the temple stand apart,

And the oak tree and the cypress grow not in each other's shadow.

And a woman who held a babe against her bosom said, Speak to us of Children.

And he said:

Your children are not your children.

They are the sons and daughters of Life's longing for itself.

They come through you but not from you,

And though they are with you yet they belong not to you.

You may give them your love but not your thoughts,

For they have their own thoughts.

You may house their bodies but not their souls,

For their souls dwell in the house of tomorrow, which you cannot visit, not even in your dreams.

You may strive to be like them, but seek not to make them like you.

For life goes not backward nor tarries with yesterday.

You are the bows from which your children as living arrows are sent forth.

The archer sees the mark upon the path of the infinite, and He bends you with His might that His arrows may go swift and far.

Let your bending in the Archer's hand be for gladness;

For even as he loves the arrow that flies, so He loves also the bow that is stable.

Then said a rich man, Speak to us of Giving.

And he answered:

You give but little when you give of your possessions.

It is when you give of yourself that you truly give.

For what are your possessions but things you keep and guard for fear you may need them tomorrow?

And tomorrow, what shall tomorrow bring to the overprudent dog burying bones in the trackless sand as he follows the pilgrims to the holy city?

And what is fear of need but need itself?

Is not dread of thirst when your well is full, the thirst that is unquenchable?

There are those who give little of the

much which they have—and they give it for recognition and their hidden desire makes their gifts unwholesome.

And there are those who have little and give it all.

These are the believers in life and the bounty of life, and their coffer is never empty.

There are those who give with joy, and that joy is their reward.

And there are those who give with pain, and that pain is their baptism.

And there are those who give and know not pain in giving, nor do they seek joy, nor give with mindfulness of virtue;

They give as in yonder valley the myrtle breathes its fragrance into space.

Through the hands of such as these God speaks, and from behind their eyes He smiles upon the earth.

It is well to give when asked, but it is better to give unasked, through understanding;

And to the open-handed the search for

one who shall receive is joy greater than giving.

And is there aught you would withhold?

All you have shall some day be given;

Therefore give now, that the season of giving may be yours and not your inheritors'.

You often say, "I would give, but only to the deserving."

The trees in your orchard say not so, nor the flocks in your pasture.

They give that they may live, for to withhold is to perish.

Surely he who is worthy to receive his days and his nights, is worthy of all else from you.

And he who has deserved to drink from the ocean of life deserves to fill his cup from your little stream.

And what desert greater shall there be, than that which lies in the courage and the confidence, nay the charity, of receiving?

And who are you that men should rend

their bosom and unveil their pride, that you may see their worth naked and their pride unabashed?

See first that you yourself deserve to be a giver, and an instrument of giving.

For in truth it is life that gives unto life—while you, who deem yourself a giver, are but a witness.

And you receivers—and you are all receivers—assume no weight of gratitude, lest you lay a yoke upon yourself and upon him who gives.

Rather rise together with the giver on his gifts as on wings;

For to be overmindful of your debt, is to doubt his generosity who has the free-hearted earth for mother, and God for father.

Then an old man, a keeper of an inn, said, Speak to us of Eating and Drinking.

And he said:

Would that you could live on the fragrance of the earth, and like an air plant be sustained by the light.

But since you must kill to eat, and rob the newly born of its mother's milk to quench your thirst, let it then be an act of worship,

And let your board stand an altar on which the pure and the innocent of forest and plain are sacrificed for that which is purer and still more innocent in man.

When you kill a beast say to him in your heart,

"By the same power that slays you, I too am slain; and I too shall be consumed.

For the law that delivered you into my hand shall deliver me into a mightier hand.

Your blood and my blood is naught but the sap that feeds the tree of heaven."

And when you crush an apple with your teeth, say to it in your heart,

"Your seeds shall live in my body,

And the buds of your tomorrow shall blossom in my heart,

And your fragrance shall be my breath,

And together we shall rejoice through all the seasons."

And in the autumn, when you gather the grapes of your vineyards for the wine-press, say in your heart,

"I too am a vineyard, and my fruit shall be gathered for the winepress,

And like new wine I shall be kept in eternal vessels."

And in winter, when you draw the wine,

28

let there be in your heart a song for each cup;

And let there be in the song a remembrance for the autumn days, and for the vineyard, and for the winepress.

Then a ploughman said, Speak to us of Work.

And he answered, saying:

You work that you may keep pace with the earth and the soul of the earth.

For to be idle is to become a stranger unto the seasons, and to step out of life's procession, that marches in majesty and proud submission towards the infinite.

When you work you are a flute through whose heart the whispering of the hours turns to music.

Which of you would be a reed, dumb and silent, when all else sings together in unison?

Always you have been told that work is a curse and labour a misfortune.

But I say to you that when you work you fulfil a part of earth's furthest dream,

30

assigned to you when that dream was born,

And in keeping yourself with labour you are in truth loving life,

And to love life through labour is to be intimate with life's inmost secret.

But if you in your pain call birth an affliction and the support of the flesh a curse written upon your brow, then I answer that naught but the sweat of your brow shall wash away that which is written.

You have been told also that life is darkness, and in your weariness you echo what was said by the weary.

And I say that life is indeed darkness save when there is urge,

And all urge is blind save when there is knowledge,

And all knowledge is vain save when there is work,

And all work is empty save when there is love;

And when you work with love you bind

yourself to yourself, and to one another, and to God.

And what is it to work with love?

It is to weave the cloth with threads drawn from your heart, even as if your beloved were to wear that cloth.

It is to build a house with affection, even as if your beloved were to dwell in that house.

It is to sow seeds with tenderness and reap the harvest with joy, even as if your beloved were to eat the fruit.

It is to charge all things you fashion with a breath of your own spirit,

And to know that all the blessed dead are standing about you and watching.

Often have I heard you say, as if speaking in sleep, "He who works in marble, and finds the shape of his own soul in the stone, is nobler than he who ploughs the soil.

And he who seizes the rainbow to lay it on a cloth in the likeness of man, is more than he who makes the sandals for our feet."

But I say, not in sleep but in the over-wakefulness of noontide, that the wind speaks not more sweetly to the giant oaks than to the least of all the blades of grass;

And he alone is great who turns the voice of the wind into a song made sweeter by his own loving.

Work is love made visible.

And if you cannot work with love but only with distaste, it is better that you should leave your work and sit at the gate of the temple and take alms of those who work with joy.

For if you bake bread with indifference, you bake a bitter bread that feeds but half man's hunger.

And if you grudge the crushing of the grapes, your grudge distils a poison in the wine.

And if you sing though as angels, and love not the singing, you muffle man's ears to the voices of the day and the voices of the night.

Then a woman said, Speak to us of Joy and Sorrow.

And he answered:

Your joy is your sorrow unmasked.

And the selfsame well from which your laughter rises was oftentimes filled with your tears.

And how else can it be?

The deeper that sorrow carves into your being, the more joy you can contain.

Is not the cup that holds your wine the very cup that was burned in the potter's oven?

And is not the lute that soothes your spirit, the very wood that was hollowed with knives?

When you are joyous, look deep into your heart and you shall find it is only that which has given you sorrow that is giving you joy.

When you are sorrowful look again in

your heart, and you shall see that in truth you are weeping for that which has been your delight.

Some of you say, "Joy is greater than sorrow," and others say, "Nay, sorrow is the greater."

But I say unto you, they are inseparable.

Together they come, and when one sits alone with you at your board, remember that the other is asleep upon your bed.

Verily you are suspended like scales between your sorrow and your joy.

Only when you are empty are you at standstill and balanced.

When the treasure-keeper lifts you to weigh his gold and his silver, needs must your joy or your sorrow rise or fall.

Then a mason came forth and said, Speak to us of Houses.

And he answered and said:

Build of your imaginings a bower in the wilderness ere you build a house within the city walls.

For even as you have home-comings in your twilight, so has the wanderer in you, the ever distant and alone.

Your house is your larger body.

It grows in the sun and sleeps in the stillness of the night; and it is not dreamless. Does not your house dream? and dreaming, leave the city for grove or hilltop?

Would that I could gather your houses into my hand, and like a sower scatter them in forest and meadow.

Would the valleys were your streets, and the green paths your alleys, that you might seek one another through vineyards, and come with the fragrance of the earth in your garments.

But these things are not yet to be.

In their fear your forefathers gathered you too near together. And that fear shall endure a little longer. A little longer shall your city walls separate your hearths from your fields.

And tell me, people of Orphalese, what have you in these houses? And what is it you guard with fastened doors?

Have you peace, the quiet urge that reveals your power?

Have you remembrances, the glimmering arches that span the summits of the mind?

Have you beauty, that leads the heart from things fashioned of wood and stone to the holy mountain?

Tell me, have you these in your houses?

Or have you only comfort, and the lust for comfort, that stealthy thing that

38

enters the house a guest, and then becomes a host, and then a master?

Ay, and it becomes a tamer, and with hook and scourge makes puppets of your larger desires.

Though its hands are silken, its heart is of iron.

It lulls you to sleep only to stand by your bed and jeer at the dignity of the flesh.

It makes mock of your sound senses, and lays them in thistledown like fragile vessels.

Verily the lust for comfort murders the passion of the soul, and then walks grinning in the funeral.

But you, children of space, you restless in rest, you shall not be trapped nor tamed.

Your house shall be not an anchor but a mast.

It shall not be a glistening film that

covers a wound, but an eyelid that guards the eye.

You shall not fold your wings that you may pass through doors, nor bend your heads that they strike not against a ceiling, nor fear to breathe lest walls should crack and fall down.

You shall not dwell in tombs made by the dead for the living.

And though of magnificence and splendour, your house shall not hold your secret nor shelter your longing.

For that which is boundless in you abides in the mansion of the sky, whose door is the morning mist, and whose windows are the songs and the silences of night.

And the weaver said, Speak to us of Clothes.

And he answered:

Your clothes conceal much of your beauty, yet they hide not the unbeautiful.

And though you seek in garments the freedom of privacy you may find in them a harness and a chain.

Would that you could meet the sun and the wind with more of your skin and less of your raiment,

For the breath of life is in the sunlight and the hand of life is in the wind.

Some of you say, "It is the north wind who has woven the clothes we wear."

And I say, Ay, it was the north wind,

But shame was his loom, and the softening of the sinews was his thread.

And when his work was done he laughed in the forest.

41

Forget not that modesty is for a shield against the eye of the unclean.

And when the unclean shall be no more, what were modesty but a fetter and a fouling of the mind?

And forget not that the earth delights to feel your bare feet and the winds long to play with your hair.

And a merchant said, Speak to us of Buying and Selling.

And he answered and said:

To you the earth yields her fruit, and you shall not want if you but know how to fill your hands.

It is in exchanging the gifts of the earth that you shall find abundance and be satisfied.

Yet unless the exchange be in love and kindly justice, it will but lead some to greed and others to hunger.

When in the market place you toilers of the sea and fields and vineyards meet the weavers and the potters and the gatherers of spices,—

Invoke then the master spirit of the earth, to come into your midst and sanctify the scales and the reckoning that weighs value against value.

43

And suffer not the barren-handed to take part in your transactions, who would sell their words for your labour.

To such men you should say,

"Come with us to the field, or go with our brothers to the sea and cast your net;

For the land and the sea shall be bountiful to you even as to us."

And if there come the singers and the dancers and the flute players,—buy of their gifts also.

For they too are gatherers of fruit and frankincense, and that which they bring, though fashioned of dreams, is raiment and food for your soul.

And before you leave the market place, see that no one has gone his way with empty hands.

For the master spirit of the earth shall not sleep peacefully upon the wind till the needs of the least of you are satisfied.

44

Then one of the judges of the city stood forth and said, Speak to us of Crime and Punishment.

And he answered, saying:

It is when your spirit goes wandering upon the wind,

That you, alone and unguarded, commit a wrong unto others and therefore unto yourself.

And for that wrong committed must you knock and wait a while unheeded at the gate of the blessed.

Like the ocean is your god-self;

It remains for ever undefiled.

And like the ether it lifts but the winged.

Even like the sun is your god-self;

It knows not the ways of the mole nor seeks it the holes of the serpent.

But your god-self dwells not alone in your being.

Much in you is still man, and much in you is not yet man,

But a shapeless pigmy that walks asleep in the mist searching for its own awakening.

And of the man in you would I now speak.

For it is he and not your god-self nor the pigmy in the mist, that knows crime and the punishment of crime.

Oftentimes have I heard you speak of one who commits a wrong as though he were not one of you, but a stranger unto you and an intruder upon your world.

But I say that even as the holy and the righteous cannot rise beyond the highest which is in each one of you,

So the wicked and the weak cannot fall lower than the lowest which is in you also.

And as a single leaf turns not yellow but with the silent knowledge of the whole tree,

46

So the wrong-doer cannot do wrong without the hidden will of you all.

Like a procession you walk together towards your god-self.

You are the way and the wayfarers.

And when one of you falls down he falls for those behind him, a caution against the stumbling stone.

Ay, and he falls for those ahead of him, who though faster and surer of foot, yet removed not the stumbling stone.

And this also, though the word lie heavy upon your hearts:

The murdered is not unaccountable for his own murder,

And the robbed is not blameless in being robbed.

The righteous is not innocent of the deeds of the wicked,

And the white-handed is not clean in the doings of the felon.

Yea, the guilty is oftentimes the victim of the injured,

And still more often the condemned is

47

the burden bearer for the guiltless and un-
blamed.

You cannot separate the just from the
unjust and the good from the wicked;

For they stand together before the face
of the sun even as the black thread and
the white are woven together.

And when the black thread breaks, the
weaver shall look into the whole cloth,
and he shall examine the loom also.

If any of you would bring to judgment
the unfaithful wife,

Let him also weigh the heart of her hus-
band in scales, and measure his soul with
measurements.

And let him who would lash the
offender look unto the spirit of the
offended.

And if any of you would punish in the
name of righteousness and lay the ax
unto the evil tree, let him see to its
roots;

And verily he will find the roots of the
good and the bad, the fruitful and the

fruitless, all entwined together in the silent heart of the earth.

And you judges who would be just,

What judgment pronounce you upon him who though honest in the flesh yet is a thief in spirit?

What penalty lay you upon him who slays in the flesh yet is himself slain in the spirit?

And how prosecute you him who in action is a deceiver and an oppressor,

Yet who also is aggrieved and outraged?

And how shall you punish those whose remorse is already greater than their misdeeds?

Is not remorse the justice which is administered by that very law which you would fain serve?

Yet you cannot lay remorse upon the innocent nor lift it from the heart of the guilty.

Unbidden shall it call in the night, that men may wake and gaze upon themselves.

And you who would understand justice, how shall you unless you look upon all deeds in the fullness of light?

Only then shall you know that the erect and the fallen are but one man standing in twilight between the night of his pigmy-self and the day of his god-self,

And that the corner-stone of the temple is not higher than the lowest stone in its foundation.

Then a lawyer said, But what of our Laws, master?

And he answered:

You delight in laying down laws,

Yet you delight more in breaking them.

Like children playing by the ocean who build sand-towers with constancy and then destroy them with laughter.

But while you build your sand-towers the ocean brings more sand to the shore,

And when you destroy them the ocean laughs with you.

Verily the ocean laughs always with the innocent.

But what of those to whom life is not an ocean, and man-made laws are not sand-towers,

But to whom life is a rock, and the law a chisel with which they would carve it in their own likeness?

What of the cripple who hates dancers?

What of the ox who loves his yoke and deems the elk and deer of the forest stray and vagrant things?

What of the old serpent who cannot shed his skin, and calls all others naked and shameless?

And of him who comes early to the wedding-feast, and when over-fed and tired goes his way saying that all feasts are violation and all feasters law-breakers?

What shall I say of these save that they too stand in the sunlight, but with their backs to the sun?

They see only their shadows, and their shadows are their laws.

And what is the sun to them but a caster of shadows?

And what is it to acknowledge the laws but to stoop down and trace their shadows upon the earth?

But you who walk facing the sun, what

images drawn on the earth can hold you?

You who travel with the wind, what weather-vane shall direct your course?

What man's law shall bind you if you break your yoke but upon no man's prison door?

What laws shall you fear if you dance but stumble against no man's iron chains?

And who is he that shall bring you to judgment if you tear off your garment yet leave it in no man's path?

People of Orphalese, you can muffle the drum, and you can loosen the strings of the lyre, but who shall command the sky-lark not to sing?

And an orator said, Speak to us of Freedom.

And he answered:

At the city gate and by your fireside I have seen you prostrate yourself and worship your own freedom,

Even as slaves humble themselves before a tyrant and praise him though he slays them.

Ay, in the grove of the temple and in the shadow of the citadel I have seen the freest among you wear their freedom as a yoke and a handcuff.

And my heart bled within me; for you can only be free when even the desire of seeking freedom becomes a harness to you, and when you cease to speak of freedom as a goal and a fulfilment.

You shall be free indeed when your days are not without a care nor your

nights without a want and a grief,
But rather when these things girdle
your life and yet you rise above them
naked and unbound.

And how shall you rise beyond your
days and nights unless you break the
chains which you at the dawn of your understanding have fastened around your
noon hour?

In truth that which you call freedom is
the strongest of these chains, though its
links glitter in the sun and dazzle your
eyes.

And what is it but fragments of your
own self you would discard that you may
become free?

If it is an unjust law you would
abolish, that law was written with your
own hand upon your own forehead.

You cannot erase it by burning your
law books nor by washing the foreheads
of your judges, though you pour the sea
upon them.

And if it is a despot you would dethrone, see first that his throne erected within you is destroyed.

For how can a tyrant rule the free and the proud, but for a tyranny in their own freedom and a shame in their own pride?

And if it is a care you would cast off, that care has been chosen by you rather than imposed upon you.

And if it is a fear you would dispel, the seat of that fear is in your heart and not in the hand of the feared.

Verily all things move within your being in constant half embrace, the desired and the dreaded, the repugnant and the cherished, the pursued and that which you would escape.

These things move within you as lights and shadows in pairs that cling.

And when the shadow fades and is no more, the light that lingers becomes a shadow to another light.

And thus your freedom when it loses its fetters becomes itself the fetter of a greater freedom.

And the priestess spoke again and said: Speak to us of Reason and Passion.

And he answered, saying:

Your soul is oftentimes a battlefield, upon which your reason and your judgment wage war against your passion and your appetite.

Would that I could be the peacemaker in your soul, that I might turn the discord and the rivalry of your elements into oneness and melody.

But how shall I, unless you yourselves be also the peacemakers, nay, the lovers of all your elements?

Your reason and your passion are the rudder and the sails of your seafaring soul.

If either your sails or your rudder be broken, you can but toss and drift, or else be held at a standstill in mid-seas.

57

For reason, ruling alone, is a force confining; and passion, unattended, is a flame that burns to its own destruction.

Therefore let your soul exalt your reason to the height of passion, that it may sing;

And let it direct your passion with reason, that your passion may live through its own daily resurrection, and like the phœnix rise above its own ashes.

I would have you consider your judgment and your appetite even as you would two loved guests in your house.

Surely you would not honour one guest above the other; for he who is more mindful of one loses the love and the faith of both

Among the hills, when you sit in the cool shade of the white poplars, sharing the peace and serenity of distant fields and meadows—then let your heart say in silence, "God rests in reason."

And when the storm comes, and the

mighty wind shakes the forest, and
thunder and lightning proclaim the
majesty of the sky,—then let your heart
say in awe, "God moves in passion."

And since you are a breath in God's
sphere, and a leaf in God's forest, you too
should rest in reason and move in passion.

And a woman spoke, saying, Tell us of Pain.

And he said:

Your pain is the breaking of the shell that encloses your understanding.

Even as the stone of the fruit must break, that its heart may stand in the sun, so must you know pain.

And could you keep your heart in wonder at the daily miracles of your life, your pain would not seem less wondrous than your joy;

And you would accept the seasons of your heart, even as you have always accepted the seasons that pass over your fields.

And you would watch with serenity through the winters of your grief.

Much of your pain is self-chosen.

It is the bitter potion by which the physician within you heals your sick self.

Therefore trust the physician, and drink his remedy in silence and tranquillity:

For his hand, though heavy and hard, is guided by the tender hand of the Unseen,

And the cup he brings, though it burn your lips, has been fashioned of the clay which the Potter has moistened with His own sacred tears.

And a man said, Speak to us of Self-Knowledge.

And he answered, saying:

Your hearts know in silence the secrets of the days and the nights.

But your ears thirst for the sound of your heart's knowledge.

You would know in words that which you have always known in thought.

You would touch with your fingers the naked body of your dreams.

And it is well you should.

The hidden well-spring of your soul must needs rise and run murmuring to the sea;

And the treasure of your infinite depths would be revealed to your eyes.

But let there be no scales to weigh your unknown treasure;

And seek not the depths of your

knowledge with staff or sounding line.

For self is a sea boundless and measure-less.

Say not, "I have found the truth," but rather, "I have found a truth."

Say not, "I have found the path of the soul." Say rather, "I have met the soul walking upon my path."

For the soul walks upon all paths.

The soul walks not upon a line, neither does it grow like a reed.

The soul unfolds itself, like a lotus of countless petals.

Then said a teacher, Speak to us of Teaching.

And he said:

No man can reveal to you aught but that which already lies half asleep in the dawning of your knowledge.

The teacher who walks in the shadow of the temple, among his followers, gives not of his wisdom but rather of his faith and his lovingness.

If he is indeed wise he does not bid you enter the house of his wisdom, but rather leads you to the threshold of your own mind.

The astronomer may speak to you of his understanding of space, but he cannot give you his understanding.

The musician may sing to you of the rhythm which is in all space, but he cannot give you the ear which arrests the rhythm nor the voice that echoes it.

And he who is versed in the science of numbers can tell of the regions of weight and measure, but he cannot conduct you thither.

For the vision of one man lends not its wings to another man.

And even as each one of you stands alone in God's knowledge, so must each one of you be alone in his knowledge of God and in his understanding of the earth.

And a youth said, Speak to us of Friendship.

And he answered, saying:

Your friend is your needs answered.

He is your field which you sow with love and reap with thanksgiving.

And he is your board and your fireside.

For you come to him with your hunger, and you seek him for peace.

When your friend speaks his mind you fear not the "nay" in your own mind, nor do you withhold the "ay."

And when he is silent your heart ceases not to listen to his heart;

For without words, in friendship, all thoughts, all desires, all expectations are born and shared, with joy that is unacclaimed.

When you part from your friend, you grieve not;

For that which you love most in him may be clearer in his absence, as the mountain to the climber is clearer from the plain.

66

And let there be no purpose in friendship save the deepening of the spirit.

For love that seeks aught but the disclosure of its own mystery is not love but a net cast forth: and only the unprofitable is caught.

And let your best be for your friend.

If he must know the ebb of your tide, let him know its flood also.

For what is your friend that you should seek him with hours to kill?

Seek him always with hours to live.

For it is his to fill your need, but not your emptiness.

And in the sweetness of friendship let there be laughter, and sharing of pleasures.

For in the dew of little things the heart finds its morning and is refreshed.

And then a scholar said, Speak of Talking.

And he answered, saying:

You talk when you cease to be at peace with your thoughts;

And when you can no longer dwell in the solitude of your heart you live in your lips, and sound is a diversion and a pastime.

And in much of your talking, thinking is half murdered.

For thought is a bird of space, that in a cage of words may indeed unfold its wings but cannot fly.

There are those among you who seek the talkative through fear of being alone.

The silence of aloneness reveals to their eyes their naked selves and they would escape.

And there are those who talk, and without knowledge or forethought reveal a truth which they themselves do not understand.

And there are those who have the truth within them, but they tell it not in words.

In the bosom of such as these the spirit dwells in rhythmic silence.

When you meet your friend on the roadside or in the market place, let the spirit in you move your lips and direct your tongue.

Let the voice within your voice speak to the ear of his ear;

For his soul will keep the truth of your heart as the taste of the wine is remembered

When the colour is forgotten and the vessel is no more.

And an astronomer said, Master, what of Time?

And he answered:

You would measure time the measureless and the immeasurable.

You would adjust your conduct and even direct the course of your spirit according to hours and seasons.

Of time you would make a stream upon whose bank you would sit and watch its flowing.

Yet the timeless in you is aware of life's timelessness,

And knows that yesterday is but today's memory and tomorrow is today's dream.

And that that which sings and contemplates in you is still dwelling within the bounds of that first moment which scattered the stars into space.

Who among you does not feel that his power to love is boundless?

And yet who does not feel that very love, though boundless, encompassed within the centre of his being, and moving not from love thought to love thought, nor from love deeds to other love deeds?

And is not time even as love is, undivided and paceless?

But if in your thought you must measure time into seasons, let each season encircle all the other seasons,

And let today embrace the past with remembrance and the future with longing.

And one of the elders of the city said, Speak to us of Good and Evil.

And he answered:

Of the good in you I can speak, but not of the evil.

For what is evil but good tortured by its own hunger and thirst?

Verily when good is hungry it seeks food even in dark caves, and when it thirsts it drinks even of dead waters.

You are good when you are one with yourself.

Yet when you are not one with yourself you are not evil.

For a divided house is not a den of thieves; it is only a divided house.

And a ship without rudder may wander aimlessly among perilous isles yet sink not to the bottom.

You are good when you strive to give of yourself.

Yet you are not evil when you seek gain for yourself.

For when you strive for gain you are but a root that clings to the earth and sucks at her breast.

Surely the fruit cannot say to the root, "Be like me, ripe and full and ever giving of your abundance."

For to the fruit giving is a need, as receiving is a need to the root.

You are good when you are fully awake in your speech,

Yet you are not evil when you sleep while your tongue staggers without purpose.

And even stumbling speech may strengthen a weak tongue.

You are good when you walk to your goal firmly and with bold steps.

Yet you are not evil when you go thither limping.

73

Even those who limp go not backward.

But you who are strong and swift, see that you do not limp before the lame, deeming it kindness.

You are good in countless ways, and you are not evil when you are not good,

You are only loitering and sluggard.

Pity that the stags cannot teach swiftness to the turtles.

In your longing for your giant self lies your goodness: and that longing is in all of you.

But in some of you that longing is a torrent rushing with might to the sea, carrying the secrets of the hillsides and the songs of the forest.

And in others it is a flat stream that loses itself in angles and bends and lingers before it reaches the shore.

But let not him who longs much say to

74

him who longs little, "Wherefore are you slow and halting?"

For the truly good ask not the naked, "Where is your garment?" nor the houseless, "What has befallen your house?"

Then a priestess said, Speak to us of Prayer.

And he answered, saying:

You pray in your distress and in your need; would that you might pray also in the fullness of your joy and in your days of abundance.

For what is prayer but the expansion of yourself into the living ether?

And if it is for your comfort to pour your darkness into space, it is also for your delight to pour forth the dawning of your heart.

And if you cannot but weep when your soul summons you to prayer, she should spur you again and yet again, though weeping, until you shall come laughing.

When you pray you rise to meet in the air those who are praying at that very hour, and whom save in prayer you may not meet.

Therefore let your visit to that temple invisible be for naught but ecstasy and sweet communion.

For if you should enter the temple for no other purpose than asking you shall not receive:

And if you should enter into it to humble yourself you shall not be lifted:

Or even if you should enter into it to beg for the good of others you shall not be heard.

It is enough that you enter the temple invisible.

I cannot teach you how to pray in words.

God listens not to your words save when He Himself utters them through your lips.

And I cannot teach you the prayer of the seas and the forests and the mountains.

But you who are born of the mountains and the forests and the seas can find their prayer in your heart,

And if you but listen in the stillness of the night you shall hear them saying in silence,

"Our God, who art our winged self, it is thy will in us that willeth.

It is thy desire in us that desireth.

It is thy urge in us that would turn our nights, which are thine, into days which are thine also.

We cannot ask thee for aught, for thou knowest our needs before they are born in us:

Thou art our need; and in giving us more of thyself thou givest us all."

Then a hermit, who visited the city once a year, came forth and said, Speak to us of Pleasure.

And he answered, saying:

Pleasure is a freedom-song,

But it is not freedom.

It is the blossoming of your desires,

But it is not their fruit.

It is a depth calling unto a height,

But it is not the deep nor the high.

It is the caged taking wing,

But it is not space encompassed.

Ay, in very truth, pleasure is a freedom-song.

And I fain would have you sing it with fullness of heart; yet I would not have you lose your hearts in the singing.

Some of your youth seek pleasure as if it were all, and they are judged and rebuked.

I would not judge nor rebuke them. I would have them seek.

For they shall find pleasure, but not her alone;

Seven are her sisters, and the least of them is more beautiful than pleasure.

Have you not heard of the man who was digging in the earth for roots and found a treasure?

And some of your elders remember pleasures with regret like wrongs committed in drunkenness.

But regret is the beclouding of the mind and not its chastisement.

They should remember their pleasures with gratitude, as they would the harvest of a summer.

Yet if it comforts them to regret, let them be comforted.

And there are among you those who are neither young to seek nor old to remember;

And in their fear of seeking and remembering they shun all pleasures, lest they neglect the spirit or offend against it.

But even in their foregoing is their pleasure.

And thus they too find a treasure though they dig for roots with quivering hands.

But tell me, who is he that can offend the spirit?

Shall the nightingale offend the still-ness of the night, or the firefly the stars?

And shall your flame or your smoke burden the wind?

Think you the spirit is a still pool which you can trouble with a staff?

Oftentimes in denying yourself pleas-ure you do but store the desire in the re-cesses of your being.

Who knows but that which seems omitted today, waits for tomorrow?

Even your body knows its heritage and its rightful need and will not be deceived.

And your body is the harp of your soul,

And it is yours to bring forth

sweet music from it or confused sounds.

And now you ask in your heart, "How shall we distinguish that which is good in pleasure from that which is not good?"

Go to your fields and your gardens, and you shall learn that it is the pleasure of the bee to gather honey of the flower,

But it is also the pleasure of the flower to yield its honey to the bee.

For to the bee a flower is a fountain of life,

And to the flower a bee is a messenger of love,

And to both, bee and flower, the giving and the receiving of pleasure is a need and an ecstasy.

People of Orphalese, be in your pleasures like the flowers and the bees.

And a poet said, Speak to us of Beauty.

And he answered:

Where shall you seek beauty, and how shall you find her unless she herself be your way and your guide?

And how shall you speak of her except she be the weaver of your speech?

The aggrieved and the injured say, "Beauty is kind and gentle.

Like a young mother half-shy of her own glory she walks among us."

And the passionate say, "Nay, beauty is a thing of might and dread.

Like the tempest she shakes the earth beneath us and the sky above us."

The tired and the weary say, "Beauty is of soft whisperings. She speaks in our spirit.

Her voice yields to our silences like a faint light that quivers in fear of the shadow."

But the restless say, "We have heard her shouting among the mountains,

And with her cries came the sound of hoofs, and the beating of wings and the roaring of lions."

At night the watchmen of the city say, "Beauty shall rise with the dawn from the east."

And at noontide the toilers and the wayfarers say, "We have seen her leaning over the earth from the windows of the sunset."

In winter say the snow-bound, "She shall come with the spring leaping upon the hills."

And in the summer heat the reapers say, "We have seen her dancing with the autumn leaves, and we saw a drift of snow in her hair."

84

All these things have you said of beauty,

Yet in truth you spoke not of her but of needs unsatisfied,

And beauty is not a need but an ecstasy.

It is not a mouth thirsting nor an empty hand stretched forth,

But rather a heart enflamed and a soul enchanted.

It is not the image you would see nor the song you would hear,

But rather an image you see though you close your eyes and a song you hear though you shut your ears.

It is not the sap within the furrowed bark, nor a wing attached to a claw,

But rather a garden for ever in bloom and a flock of angels for ever in flight.

People of Orphalese, beauty is life when life unveils her holy face.

But you are life and you are the veil.

85

Beauty is eternity gazing at itself in a mirror.

But you are eternity and you are the mirror.

And an old priest said, Speak to us of Religion.

And he said:

Have I spoken this day of aught else?

Is not religion all deeds and all reflection,

And that which is neither deed nor reflection, but a wonder and a surprise ever springing in the soul, even while the hands hew the stone or tend the loom?

Who can separate his faith from his actions, or his belief from his occupations?

Who can spread his hours before him, saying, "This for God and this for myself; This for my soul, and this other for my body?"

All your hours are wings that beat through space from self to self.

87

He who wears his morality but as his best garment were better naked.

The wind and the sun will tear no holes in his skin.

And he who defines his conduct by ethics imprisons his song-bird in a cage.

The freest song comes not through bars and wires.

And he to whom worshipping is a window, to open but also to shut, has not yet visited the house of his soul whose windows are from dawn to dawn.

Your daily life is your temple and your religion.

Whenever you enter into it take with you your all.

Take the plough and the forge and the mallet and the lute,

The things you have fashioned in necessity or for delight.

For in revery you cannot rise above your achievements nor fall lower than your failures.

And take with you all men:

For in adoration you cannot fly higher than their hopes nor humble yourself lower than their despair.

And if you would know God be not therefore a solver of riddles.

Rather look about you and you shall see Him playing with your children.

And look into space; you shall see Him walking in the cloud, outstretching His arms in the lightning and descending in rain.

You shall see Him smiling in flowers, then rising and waving His hands in trees.

Then Almitra spoke, saying, We would ask now of Death.

And he said:

You would know the secret of death.

But how shall you find it unless you seek it in the heart of life?

The owl whose night-bound eyes are blind unto the day cannot unveil the mystery of light.

If you would indeed behold the spirit of death, open your heart wide unto the body of life.

For life and death are one, even as the river and the sea are one.

In the depth of your hopes and desires lies your silent knowledge of the beyond;

And like seeds dreaming beneath the snow your heart dreams of spring.

Trust the dreams, for in them is hidden the gate to eternity.

90

Your fear of death is but the trembling of the shepherd when he stands before the king whose hand is to be laid upon him in honour.

Is the shepherd not joyful beneath his trembling, that he shall wear the mark of the king?

Yet is he not more mindful of his trembling?

For what is it to die but to stand naked in the wind and to melt into the sun?

And what is it to cease breathing, but to free the breath from its restless tides, that it may rise and expand and seek God unencumbered?

Only when you drink from the river of silence shall you indeed sing.

And when you have reached the mountain top, then you shall begin to climb.

And when the earth shall claim your limbs, then shall you truly dance.

And now it was evening.

And Almitra the seeress said, Blessed be this day and this place and your spirit that has spoken.

And he answered, Was it I who spoke? Was I not also a listener?

Then he descended the steps of the Temple and all the people followed him. And he reached his ship and stood upon the deck.

And facing the people again, he raised his voice and said:

People of Orphalese, the wind bids me leave you.

Less hasty am I than the wind, yet I must go.

We wanderers, ever seeking the lonelier way, begin no day where we have ended another day; and no sunrise finds us where sunset left us.

Even while the earth sleeps we travel.

We are the seeds of the tenacious plant, and it is in our ripeness and our fullness of heart that we are given to the wind and are scattered.

Brief were my days among you, and briefer still the words I have spoken.

But should my voice fade in your ears, and my love vanish in your memory, then I will come again,

And with a richer heart and lips more yielding to the spirit will I speak.

Yea, I shall return with the tide,

And though death may hide me, and the greater silence enfold me, yet again will I seek your understanding.

And not in vain will I seek.

If aught I have said is truth, that truth shall reveal itself in a clearer voice, and in words more kin to your thoughts.

I go with the wind, people of Orphalese, but not down into emptiness;

And if this day is not a fulfilment of your needs and my love, then let it be a promise till another day.

Man's needs change, but not his love, nor his desire that his love should satisfy his needs.

Know therefore, that from the greater silence I shall return.

The mist that drifts away at dawn, leaving but dew in the fields, shall rise and gather into a cloud and then fall down in rain.

And not unlike the mist have I been.

In the stillness of the night I have walked in your streets, and my spirit has entered your houses,

And your heart-beats were in my heart, and your breath was upon my face, and I knew you all.

Ay, I knew your joy and your pain, and in your sleep your dreams were my dreams.

And oftentimes I was among you a lake among the mountains.

I mirrored the summits in you and the

bending slopes, and even the passing flocks of your thoughts and your desires.

And to my silence came the laughter of your children in streams, and the longing of your youths in rivers.

And when they reached my depth the streams and the rivers ceased not yet to sing.

But sweeter still than laughter and greater than longing came to me.

It was the boundless in you;

The vast man in whom you are all but cells and sinews;

He in whose chant all your singing is but a soundless throbbing.

It is in the vast man that you are vast,

And in beholding him that I beheld you and loved you.

For what distances can love reach that are not in that vast sphere?

What visions, what expectations and what presumptions can outsoar that flight?

Like a giant oak tree covered with apple blossoms is the vast man in you.

His might binds you to the earth, his fragrance lifts you into space, and in his durability you are deathless.

You have been told that, even like a chain, you are as weak as your weakest link.

This is but half the truth. You are also as strong as your strongest link.

To measure you by your smallest deed is to reckon the power of ocean by the frailty of its foam.

To judge you by your failures is to cast blame upon the seasons for their inconstancy.

Ay, you are like an ocean,
And though heavy-grounded ships await the tide upon your shores, yet, even like an ocean, you cannot hasten your tides.

And like the seasons you are also,
And though in your winter you deny your spring,
Yet spring, reposing within you, smiles in her drowsiness and is not offended.

Think not I say these things in order that you may say the one to the other, "He praised us well. He saw but the good in us."

I only speak to you in words of that which you yourselves know in thought.

And what is word knowledge but a shadow of wordless knowledge?

Your thoughts and my words are waves from a sealed memory that keeps records of our yesterdays,

And of the ancient days when the earth knew not us nor herself,

And of nights when earth was up-wrought with confusion.

Wise men have come to you to give you of their wisdom. I came to take of your wisdom:

And behold I have found that which is greater than wisdom.

It is a flame spirit in you ever gathering more of itself,

While you, heedless of its expansion, bewail the withering of your days.

It is life in quest of life in bodies that fear the grave.

There are no graves here.
These mountains and plains are a cradle and a stepping-stone.
Whenever you pass by the field where you have laid your ancestors look well thereupon, and you shall see yourselves and your children dancing hand in hand.
Verily you often make merry without knowing.

Others have come to you to whom for golden promises made unto your faith you have given but riches and power and glory.
Less than a promise have I given, and yet more generous have you been to me.
You have given me my deeper thirsting after life.
Surely there is no greater gift to a man than that which turns all his aims into parching lips and all life into a fountain.

And in this lies my honour and my reward,—

That whenever I come to the fountain to drink I find the living water itself thirsty;

And it drinks me while I drink it.

Some of you have deemed me proud and over-shy to receive gifts.

Too proud indeed am I to receive wages, but not gifts.

And though I have eaten berries among the hills when you would have had me sit at your board,

And slept in the portico of the temple when you would gladly have sheltered me,

Yet was it not your loving mindfulness of my days and my nights that made food sweet to my mouth and girdled my sleep with visions?

For this I bless you most:

You give much and know not that you give at all.

Verily the kindness that gazes upon itself in a mirror turns to stone,

And a good deed that calls itself by tender names becomes the parent to a curse.

And some of you have called me aloof,
and drunk with my own aloneness,

And you have said, "He holds council
with the trees of the forest, but not with
men.

He sits alone on hill-tops and looks
down upon our city."

True it is that I have climbed the hills
and walked in remote places.

How could I have seen you save from
a great height or a great distance?

How can one be indeed near unless he
be far?

And others among you called unto me,
not in words, and they said,

"Stranger, stranger, lover of unreach-
able heights, why dwell you among the
summits where eagles build their nests?

Why seek you the unattainable?

What storms would you trap in your net,

And what vaporous birds do you hunt in the sky?

Come and be one of us.

Descend and appease your hunger with our bread and quench your thirst with our wine."

In the solitude of their souls they said these things;

But were their solitude deeper they would have known that I sought but the secret of your joy and your pain,

And I hunted only your larger selves that walk the sky.

But the hunter was also the hunted;

For many of my arrows left my bow only to seek my own breast.

And the flier was also the creeper;

For when my wings were spread in the sun their shadow upon the earth was a turtle.

And I the believer was also the doubter;

For often have I put my finger in my own wound that I might have the greater belief in you and the greater knowledge of you.

And it is with this belief and this knowledge that I say,
You are not enclosed within your bodies, nor confined to houses or fields.
That which is you dwells above the mountain and roves with the wind.
It is not a thing that crawls into the sun for warmth or digs holes into darkness for safety,
But a thing free, a spirit that envelops the earth and moves in the ether.

If these be vague words, then seek not to clear them.
Vague and nebulous is the beginning of all things, but not their end,
And I fain would have you remember me as a beginning.
Life, and all that lives, is conceived in the mist and not in the crystal.

102

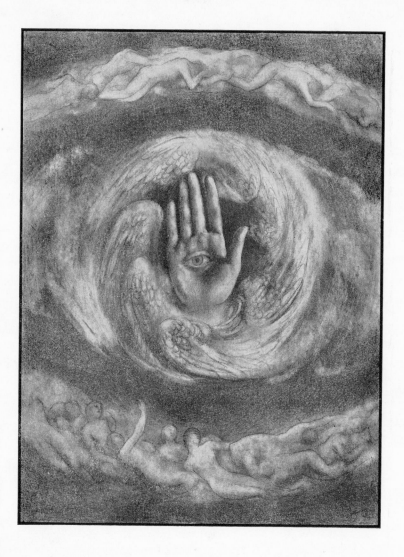

the ship until it had vanished into the mist.

And when all the people were dispersed she still stood alone upon the sea-wall, remembering in her heart his saying,

"A little while, a moment of rest upon the wind, and another woman shall bear me."

A NOTE ON THE TYPE
IN WHICH THIS BOOK IS SET

• • •

This book is set (on the Linotype) in Original Old Style. Of the history of it very little is known; in practically its present form, it has been used for many years for fine book and magazine work. Original Old Style possesses in a high degree those two qualities by which a book type must be judged; first legibility, and second, the ability to impart a definite character to a page without intruding itself upon the reader's consciousness.

PRINTED AND BOUND BY THE PLIMPTON PRESS,
NORWOOD, MASS.

PEOPLE OF THE BREAKING DAY

written and illustrated by Marcia Sewall

Atheneum   1990   New York

92100

ACKNOWLEDGMENTS

I wish to thank Daisy Moore—Whispering Waters—of Mingo/Mye, Inc., for her helpful suggestions; Barbara Norton and Theresa Furfey, who gave me invaluable material at the beginning of this journey; friends at the Codman Square Branch of the Boston Public Library for their gracious assistance; Pat Cleaveland for her time and encouragement; The Workshop group; my editor, Marcia Marshall, for her good judgment; my mother, for sharing her love of nature with me; and Peter, my Sunday landscape painting friend, for our many excursions to look at sunlight and shadow.

The quote on page 3 is found in Indian New England Before the Mayflower, *by Howard S. Russell, published by University Press of New England.*

Atheneum
Macmillan Publishing Company
866 Third Avenue, New York, NY 10022
Collier Macmillan Canada, Inc.
First Edition
Printed in Hong Kong
10   9   8   7   6   5   4   3   2   1

T 50697

Library of Congress Cataloging-in-Publication Data
Sewall, Marcia.
People of the breaking day / by Marcia Sewall.
—1st ed.   p.   cm.
Summary: a poetic evocation of the life-style and traditional
beliefs of the Wampanoag Indians.
ISBN 0-689-31407-8
1. Wampanoag Indians—Juvenile literature. [1. Wampanoag
Indians. 2. Indians of North America.] I. Title.
E99.W2S49   1990   305.8'973—dc20
89-18194   CIP   AC

In memory of Steve Howe

"With all beings and all things we shall be as brothers."

OUR TRIBE

We are Wampanoags, People of the Breaking Day. Nippa'uus, the Sun, on his journey through the sky, warms us first as he rises over the rim of the sea. At his birth each new morning we say, "Thank you, Nippa'uus, for returning to us with your warmth and light and beauty."

But it is Kiehtan, the Great Spirit, who made us all: we, the two-legged who stand tall, and the four-legged; those that swim and those that fly and the little people who crawl; and flowers and trees and rocks. He made us all, brothers sharing the earth. From the birds and beasts and fish, we, the two-legged, will each choose a guardian spirit, our manitou for life.

We who stand tall admire the keen sight of the hawk. We have learned to sweep the woods with our eyes and catch movement there. We appreciate the stealth of the fox as he stalks his prey, and we, too, have learned to tread silently. We know the tracks left by animal footprints and have learned how to hide our own. We respect the four-leggeds' keen sense of smell, for they always know our whereabouts unless we smoke our bodies by burning sage or sweet grass. And, like fish, we swim.

5

We are a nation of people, a large family of several thousand people. We speak the same language. We worship the same spirits. We live in small settlements never too far from the sea, where the sun rises.

Our many villages are within a day's run of each other. Paths, like sinew, bind them together. The people of our villages may hunt and fish together in season. For planting, we may gather to help each other break up fields. And how much we look forward to spring—warm days again

and plentiful food again! Then we will come together to celebrate a season of plenty.

When corn silks darken in the Neepunnakee'wush moon, once more we shall gather to celebrate this gift of food. We will build a dance house many, many feet long and, for a week, dance and sing and play games together and eat plenty, but first we will place a pot of precious corn on the hot coals to burn and, in smoke, to mingle with the spirit powers.

It was Crow who came to us long ago from the direction of the warm wind, home of Kiehtan, the Great Spirit, carrying a corn seed and a bean seed in his ears. We thank him for his gifts. No longer must we roam about the earth always searching for food. Now we plant a garden.

Every year when the Sequanakee'wush moon comes around again, and warm rains fall upon the earth again, and the Thunder Beings shake the sky, it is planting time. If warm rains stop falling and our seeds

do not grow, we will climb the sacred hill and pray to the Great Spirit and ask him to favor us with rain. And if the sun does not shine, we will climb the sacred hill and ask the Great Spirit to favor us with sun. If he is pleased with us, rain will follow sun and sun will follow rain. Our seeds will grow and we shall have food. Then we will survive when cold winds howl and snow blankets the earth, when bears sleep and we grow lean.

Our great sachem is Massasoit, a man of peace, who became our leader upon his father's death. And so it will be. For Wamsutta, Massasoit's oldest son, one day shall lead our people. Our great sachem knows the fields and forests and waters where our tribe can hunt and fish and grow crops. He decides upon our just punishment if the rules of our people are broken. And it is our great sachem and his council of warriors who decide when we should make war. Lesser sachems advise our great leader of the needs of each small settlement within the large Wampanoag nation.

Narragansetts and Nausets, Nipmucks and Massachusetts, Pequots and Niantics are other tribes that live near us, with their own sachems and their own lands for hunting and fishing. Farther away live Penacooks and Abanakis, Mohawks and Mahicans. We are sometimes at war with each other and sometimes at peace. Our braves may fight for a good hunting ground or fishing stream or berry patch, and they are quick to avenge a wrong deed. When our sons are sixteen winters old and have proved their bravery, they can become warriors.

In preparation for war, we who are warriors paint ourselves fiercely. We mix colors with animal grease to make paint: black from charcoal; red, in springtime, from the juice of bloodroot plants and, in fall, from black currant berries; white from clay found in the riverbed; and green from young shoots of elder bushes.

The night before a battle, we dance a dance of war and beat the ground with sticks and pierce the sky with war cries. Our pulses quicken. At dawn we drink a strong juniper-berry tea to help our blood clot if we should be wounded. Then we ask the spirit powers to make us

swift as the deer, cunning as the fox, and may our poisoned arrows find their marks. We are ready to fight.

Since boyhood we have been trained to be proud and courageous; to run many miles a day; to endure pain and cold and tainted foods; to be calm and silent and strong. If wounded, like our animal brothers we will lie with our wound against Mother Earth and she will try to heal us. If captured, we are prepared to suffer and die. We are proud of our bravery. For a great coup a warrior will place another eagle feather in his shiny black hair.

When at peace we eagerly trade with other people. We especially prize the Narragansetts' soapstone pipes and bowls and wampum; delicate purple and white beads made from quahog shells found in their waters. We trade these pipes and bowls and beads, and our own wooden bowls and corn seed with the Abanakis north of us for their birch bark, which we will make into lightweight canoes. And we will trade what we have with people many sleeps away for their pretty fire-lit copper and their sharp-cutting flints.

In peacetime, we play fair games with the other nations. Our men love to gather in a crowd and gamble. *"Hub! Hub! Hub!"* they cry, hoping for a winning throw of their black-and-white bone dice. On vast distances of sand by the sea, our men, disguised in war paint, play a rough game of ball. It may take days, and even a few broken bones, before the ball is kicked over a goalpost and the game won! We love a good footrace and we enjoy matching our skill with bows and arrows. When our games are over, we say *"Hawu'nshech"* and part as peaceful neighbors.

A FAMILY

Our father, brave and strong and wise, is always our gentle teacher. He observes Nippa'uus, the Sun, and Munna'mock, the Moon, and the stars. He feels the Wind Spirits as they change places. He, at all times, watches the shape of clouds and the colors of the sea. As a brother of all plants and animals, he knows them well and with great knowledge makes decisions that will affect our lives. When and where we move is most important to the survival of our family. If we go to high land, we will see all that is about us. If our village is surrounded by swamp, then we are well hidden from our enemies. But wherever we go, there must be firewood nearby. He talks about these matters with the leader of our village, who then holds council with the leader of our tribe.

Much time our father spends making arrows from hardwood saplings with points carefully shaped of bone or flint or eagle claw; and bows, tall as a man, from strong, flexible wood strung with sinew. Many days he will prepare for the hunt. For a deer drive, miles of fence must be cut and put in place so that the deer will run to a small opening and into his swift arrows. For trapping, snares must be laid. For fishing, he must shape hooks and spears from bone and wood. From hemp, twisted and braided, he makes fish line. He will weave purse nets for scooping up fish, and long gill nets in which to entangle them. He will make a

mishoo'n shaped from a tall chestnut or pine tree. Slowly he will burn and scrape and hollow the wood, making a gouge fit for men to sit in. Then he will paddle out onto the open sea or down the beautiful rivers, there to catch fish.

He will cut long sapling poles, pound them into the earth, then bend and tie them together to make the frame of our *wetu*. And the men of our village will build a smokehouse and a sweat lodge. Men leave the labor of gardening to women, except for their prized plots of *ottomma'ocke*.

Our mother cares for our needs and is patient with us as we grow. It is she who tends our planting fields. It is she who prepares and preserves our food. Her capable hands turn deerskin into clothes and weave our mats and baskets. Her strong back carries our shelter and belongings from place to place, and we, her daughters, help her. We love to listen to her songs, full of thanks for life and for earth's gifts.

We, the children of our family, roam over the fields and along the shore. We play in the brook and we are constantly in and out of the pond. We especially like to skirt the edges of the forest and make small wigwams there. We are eager to know about everything that we see and hear and smell.

In the Namassackee'wush moon, when river ice has gone, when ducks and geese return to Father Sky and bring back the east wind that melts the snow, it is time for our family to return to the fishing place. Fish, again, will swim from the deep sea up the swift-moving rivers and over the falls to lay their eggs. Our men now catch them in their purse nets. It is a time of plenty.

Now our mother will move our belongings from the wintering place to the fishing stream and, soon, on to the planting fields as the days lengthen. On her back in a cradleboard rides a little *papoo's*, coated with a layer of animal grease for warmth and wrapped in soft skins. Only our family and the leaders of our tribe will know her true name, for names are sacred. People will call her by her nickname, Little Sweet Red Berry.

When we arrive at the planting fields, our first job, as children, is

to fetch water from the spring nearby. Then, after we collect firewood, one of the boys will make a dancing flame with his fire bow and light the dry kindling. There will be fish in the stream not far away and plenty of squirrels in the trees and perhaps a foraging turkey to be hunted. At the shore nearby there are clams to be dug. Now our mother will put together a meal, for we are hungry! Into the pot of cooking food she will throw a little cornmeal for nourishment and thickening, and some clam broth for flavoring.

Setting up our *wetu* this spring will not be difficult, for the bent sapling poles, used last year, still remain standing beside the planting fields. Our mother will lash cattail-stem wall coverings to those poles with cord she has made from pounded and twisted bark, leaving a low opening for a door. Next, she will cover the inside walls with mats carefully woven of bulrushes, and on the tamped-down earth place mats for us to sleep upon. In time, our father may make some low bed racks. Though at the top of our *wetu* is a smoke hole, there are days when our dwelling is smoky and our eyes burn. Often we prefer to sleep with our animal brothers under the night sky.

When white oak leaves bud, it is time for our mother again to set corn. If there is little new spring growth in the old cornfield, we know the earth is tired. Then our father will clear more land with his stone ax and sacred fire and make another sunny garden place for growing seeds.

Last year, as always, our mother saved out the best formed ears of *ewa'chim* for seed, pulled back the husks, and braided them together, allowing them to dry. During three moons she will plant those seeds. For three moons she will harvest them. In each small mound of earth, hoed with a quahog-shell hoe, she will first place herring or chopped-up horseshoe crabs to rot and nourish the soil. Within a double handful of sleeps, with her planting stick barely disturbing Mother Earth, she will poke holes in the soil and plant, in each mound, four corn and two bean seeds. Nearby she will plant a patch of pumpkins.

We, the children of our family, will spend our days now at the

planting fields, for we must shoo away birds who come to feast on the newly planted seeds. But we are always careful not to harm our friend Crow.

Our garden is easy to tend. As cornstalks grow tall, sprouting beans will climb the stalks and reach for sun. In between the hills of corn, our mother plants squash and cucumber seeds. They will spread their broad leaves across the warm earth, holding moisture in the soil and keeping weeds down. We listen at night to the dogs barking. They are hunting raccoons in our cornfield. We are grateful for their watchful spirit.

Now it is time to help our mother dig clay from the riverbed. The sun is hot on our backs and we happily swim to wash off. Then we must drag the heavy clay home. We watch the women of our village knead the clay and shape it into beautiful pots, then take a scrap of shell and carefully draw a pattern into the hardening surface. We can't resist taking a bit of clay to make a few dogs and dolls and a dugout canoe. After we dry what we have made, we put those things on hot coals to harden them.

Our mother often goes to the shore to dig clams and we, who are

her daughters, help her. In preparation for winter, we will cook the shucked *sicki'ssuog* on sweet green sticks over an open fire. We will also spear and roast large crabs and lobsters, and dry fish on racks in the sun or smoke them in smokehouses, along with eels and animal flesh. The smell of the delicious smoked foods fills our heads. We taste a bit of everything and store the rest. In red cedar baskets and animal-skin bags, deep in earth pits dug by our men, we will bury our preserved food. Let the cold winds bite! Let snow fall deep around our winter dwelling! We know what Mother Earth holds for us.

29

During the growing season we who are women, young and old, gather plants for medicine and for food. We know just where we can find groundnuts and wild rice and sea lettuce, which we will add to a nourishing stew. In the woods we know where to find shiny wintergreen leaves, which we will grind fine and mix with animal grease to be rubbed into the aching joints of our old people. In baskets we gather many sorts of bark. Our bonesetter will make splints of heavy bark, and birch bark and pine bark are soothing to burns.

We who are children love to dive for water-lily roots to be dried and pounded into a healing powder. Nearby we pull up skunk cabbage. Formed into a poultice, it is good for toothaches! In the forest we collect acorns from the white oak tree, and chestnuts, and in sunny places we look for berries. Strawberries grow as large as our small hands.

As harvesttime nears, we spend days gathering cattails and hemp and grasses and flexible woods, which we will boil and dry, then weave into mats and wall coverings and baskets of all shapes and sizes.

When the locusts begin to sing, we know that we will have no more than a few handfuls of sleeps before the first frost comes. We must then be sure to gather in our corn and pumpkins, squashes and cucumbers and beans. We thank you, Spirit of the Locust, for your gentle warning.

Throughout the next moons, we, the women of our family, will roast corn and dry corn and grind it into samp, which we will boil with berries. We will make it into bread and pound it into journey-cake meal and parch it and pound it into nourishing nocake meal, which our men always carry tucked into their belt pouches. And, we love the corn that pops! We will mix corn with beans and make succotash. We will throw whole ears of corn, with fish and *sicki'ssuog*, onto stones made hot by fire and bake them under seaweed. We are grateful to you, Crow, for your gift of corn seed.

When the wind beats cold upon our bodies, and again *ho'nckock* and *quequecumau'og* fly away, we, the men of our family, will hunt deer. Like ourselves, deer are fattest at harvesttime. Not only do we need their meat to smoke and dry for winter food, but we must have their skins for clothing, their bladders for bags, their bones for sewing needles and fishhooks, and their tendons for our sinew threads. We are careful to waste nothing that the deer gives to us. We kill only what we need.

Now, when Munna'mock, the Moon, rises round and full, we know it is time for us to catch eels, for they are beginning to swim from the

pond out to sea under the cover of darkness. We will narrow the river with bushes and place our eel traps there to catch them as they pass through the small opening. Thank you, Great Spirit, for making it so.

We have watched the beaver build his dam and his lodge and we know where to find him if we are hungry. Then we will trap him and eat his meat and roast his fat tail and use his fur for warmth. But we are always careful to return his bones to his familiar stream, where, we know, as a beaver, he will live again.

At Pepe'warr, the time of white frost, when leaves sink to the earth in their bright colors, our family returns inland. Away from strong, cold sea winds, our winter longhouse nestles into the protection of a sunny hillside with the forest nearby. Now, the women of the families who share the longhouse will place flattened slabs of dried bark on top of the

woven mats covering the dwelling—another layer to shelter us from the oncoming cold.

As fresh water freezes into thick ice on lakes and ponds, men will chop round holes in the ice and through them spear fish.

It is now that we who are soon to become men are taken blindfolded into the deep forest to be left alone there for the winter with our bow and arrows, a knife and a hatchet, and that is all. As boys we have learned much about survival from our fathers. Still, we will nearly freeze and starve if the winter moons are harsh ones. We will have dreams which, in time, the medicine man will help us understand. We will grow strong and unyielding to cold and pain and hunger. We will learn to know animals as brothers. If we are humbled and made wise, we will grow into leaders of our tribe. Some of us will now become warriors.

Inside the longhouse each of our families is warmed by a fire. When snow and rain keep men from scouring the forest for food, they will spend hours carefully chipping stone against stone to make arrowheads and hatchets. *Muckachuck* will shape arrowheads and hatchets, too. Women will weave dried grasses, stored since summer, into mats and baskets and will pound and twist bark into string and turn animal skins into warm clothing. *Nunsqua*, too, will weave and make string and learn to sew.

If there is food, we will have a pot cooking over the open fire. These are often pleasant hours, filled with good talk and laughter. We are happy living close together, sharing food, sleeping on simple rack beds near the fire. We lie close to one another, with bearskin blankets thrown over our greased and glistening bodies. We love to listen to the old stories of our tribe told by our elders during the long, dark hours. In sleep, we hope for dreams that will give us wisdom. Outside, the Wind Spirits howl and snow blows about us. *Tauh coi!*

We live as our grandfathers' grandfathers have lived forever, rising each day with the rebirth of Nippa'uus, to eat when hungry, to sleep when tired, to gather for celebration, to glean food and do our planting. We, the two-legged, are all equal except for our leader and the shaman, our medicine man. Magic flows through the medicine man like a river connecting what we see to what we cannot see. We cannot see what makes the rain fall. We cannot see what makes a person die. Spirits are everywhere, in everything, and we try not to anger them. If we do, it is the medicine man with his mysterious chants and his medicine bag who comes to help us. Gratefully we pay him with gifts of corn and animal skins and precious beads for his efforts to heal us and keep evil spirits away from our homes.

When we die, we will be wrapped in furs or mats and buried in the evening facing the setting sun with our *mocu'ssinass* in our hands. At our feet will be placed a pot of water; at our head, a basket of meat. These we will need for our journey to the land of Kiehtan, the land where Crow

came from. Those who survive us will blacken their faces and mourn and leave our house empty forever, never to mention our name again. So it has been. So it will always be.

Aque'ne

GLOSSARY

AVENGE—to strike back

BARK—outer layer of a tree

BLADDER—a sac within an animal, which holds body fluids; used by man as containers and balls

BULRUSH—a variety of tall grassy plants that grow in wet places

CATTAIL—a marsh plant having long, straplike leaves and a tall stem

CEDAR—an evergreen tree with an odor unpleasant to insects

CLAM—a type of shellfish

COPPER—a reddish brown metal that is easy to shape into ornaments

CORN SILKS—the tassles found on the tops of ears of corn

COUP—victory

DAY'S RUN—a strong messenger's one-day run, about one hundred miles

FIRE BOW—a friction device used for starting a fire

FLINT—stone that can be easily chipped to a knifelike edge

GLEAN—scrape together

GREEN STICK—a young stick still full of the moisture that prevents it from burning

GROUNDNUT—an edible root that looks like a potato

HEMP—a tall plant with a coarse fiber that can be twisted into string and braided into rope

HERRING—a saltwater fish, small in size

HORSESHOE CRAB—shellfish having a large shelled body and stiff pointed tail

HUSK—the outer covering of an ear of corn

KINDLING—dry sticks of wood that will burn easily

KNEAD—to press and shape with your hands into an even mass

LASH—to tie securely in place

LITTLE PEOPLE—insects

LONGHOUSE—a winter dwelling used by Native Americans in the Northeast, which would shelter from four to eight families, depending on its size

MEDICINE BAG—pouch carried by the medicine man. It held plants, sticks, whistles, and perhaps some part of an animal, which he would magically call upon to cure the sick.

MEDICINE MAN—a person gifted with spiritual powers

MOONS—a means of telling time by months

MOURN—to feel sadness at the death of a loved one

PARCH—to roast over hot ashes

POULTICE—moist mass applied to inflamed part of the body

QUAHOG—large clam

SAGE—strong-smelling plant

SAMP—corn porridge

SAPLING—young tree

SHAMAN—medicine man, a spiritual leader of the tribe

SHUCKED CLAM—clam removed from its shell

SINEW—animal tendons, chewed till soft, then twisted into thread or bowstrings and lashings

SMOKEHOUSE—a temporary structure with open ends, containing racks to hold fish and flesh to be preserved by smoking over an open fire

SNARE—a loop of strong twine assembled to catch animals attracted to some deliberately set food

SOAPSTONE—a stone that can be carved

SWEAT LODGE—a hut with a stone floor on which a fire is built. When the stones are hot, ashes are swept outside and water is poured over the hot stones, creating steam. After an hour of sweating, people leave the sweat lodge and jump into a cold stream or lake nearby. Good for the health.

SWEET GRASS—a sweet-smelling grass

TAINTED—poisoned

TAMPED-DOWN—earth pounded firm

TENDON—a tough tissue that connects bones and muscles

WAMPUM—shell beads used as jewelry and money

WIGWAM—cone- or domed-shaped shelter used by Native Americans of the Northeast

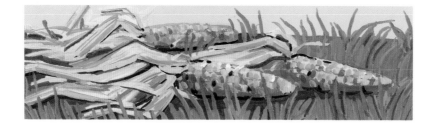

WAMPANOAG / NARRAGANSETT
NATIVE AMERICAN WORDS

aque'ne—peace
ewa'chim—corn
"Hawu'nshech"—"Good-bye"
ho'nckock—geese
"Hub! Hub! Hub!"—"Come! Come! Come!"
mishoo'n—dugout canoe
mocu'ssinass—moccasins, deerskin shoes
muckachuck—boys
Namassackee'wush—March, April; the time of
    catching fish
Neepunnakee'wush—August, September; when
    corn is edible

nunsqua—girls
ottomma'ocke—tobacco
papoo's—papoose
Pepe'warr—October, November; white frost
quequecumau'og—ducks
Sequanakee'wush—late April, early May; time to
    set corn
sicki'ssuog—clams
"Tauh coi!"—"It is very cold!"
wetu—house